D0410453

BBC CHILDREN'S BOOKS
Published by the Penguin Group
Penguin Books Ltd, 80 Strand, London WC2R 0RL, England
Penguin Group (Australia), 250 Camberwell Road, Camberwell, Victoria 3124,
Australia (a division of Pearson Australia Group Pty Ltd)
First published by BBC Worldwide Ltd, 2000
Text and design © BBC Children's Character Books, 2000
This edition published by BBC Children's Books, 2006
CBeebies & logo™ BBC. © BBC 2002
BBC & logo © and ™ BBC 1996
10 9 8 7 6 5 4 3 2 1
Written by Diane Redmond
Based upon the television series
Bob the Builder © 2006 HIT Entertainment Ltd. and Keith Chapman.
The Bob the Builder name and character and the Wendy, Spud, Roley,
Muck, Pilchard, Dizzy, Lofty and Scoop characters are trademarks of
HIT Entertainment Ltd. Registered in the UK.
With thanks to HOT Animation
www.bobthebuilder.com
All rights reserved.
ISBN 1 40590181 0
Printed in Italy

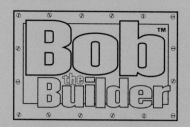

Can Spud Fix It?

BBC
CHILDREN'S BOOKS

It was early morning in Bob's Building Yard. Bob was getting ready to go to the pond and put up a new sign.

"Here's your toolbox," said Wendy, as she passed him the heavy box.

Bob climbed aboard Scoop. "Let's go,"
he said leading Lofty and Dizzy out of
the yard.

Down the road, Spud was complaining to Travis.

"Being a scarecrow isn't as easy as you think," he grumbled.

Suddenly the old gate that he was leaning against gave way and Spud fell over.

"Right, that's it!" said Spud crossly. "I'm going to get a new job. I could be a pilot!"

"You can't fly!" laughed Travis.

"I could learn," insisted Spud. Spreading his arms like aeroplane wings, he flapped them up and down.

Just then, Bob and the machines came chugging around the corner and almost crashed into Spud.

"Look out!" yelled Bob. Scoop slammed on his brakes sending Bob's toolbox flying.

"Spud! You should never play near roads! Now, please go and tell Farmer Pickles that I won't be able to fix the window frames in the old cottage until tomorrow. Thank you," cried Bob, as he headed off to the pond.

"Yes, Bob. Sorry, Bob," muttered Spud.

Spud saw Bob's toolbox on the road.

"Forget Spud the Scarecrow!" he cried as he pulled out a bright shiny spanner. "From now on I'm Spud the Spanner! I'm going to be a builder just like Bob!"

Then Spud pulled out a hammer and started to mend the gate. "This building stuff is easy!" he giggled. "I think I'll go and fix the cottage windows next."

When Bob got to the duck pond he discovered that his toolbox was missing.

"My favourite spanner is in it," he moaned.

Bob asked Lofty to go back and see if the toolbox had fallen out during the journey.

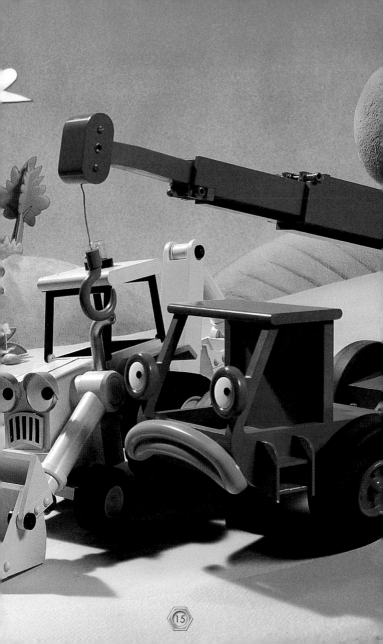

As Lofty was looking for Bob's toolbox, he bumped into Spud, who was carrying the toolbox.

"Er, Spud," Lofty said nervously, "that's Bob's toolbox. Can I have it back, please?"

"Only if you help me with a bit of building first," said Spud.

Lofty didn't really like the idea but he agreed to help.

"Hurray!" yelled Spud. "I've got a machine. Now I'm a proper builder!"

At the pond Bob waited and waited for Lofty. He decided to phone Wendy to get her to send Muck over with his spare toolbox.

On his way over, Muck bumped into Lofty and Spud.

"We're off to fix the cottage windows," shouted Spud, as they sped past.

Muck rushed to the pond.

"Bob! Bob!" Muck cried. "Lofty and Spud are on their way to the old cottage with your toolbox!"

"Let's go team!" said Bob. "We've got to stop Spud before he hurts himself."

At the old cottage, Spud admired the
work he had done. "Not a bad job!" he
said proudly.

Lofty clanked nervously. "Oh, er, but...
erm... all the windows are crooked!"

"That's how they're supposed to look!"
laughed Spud. "Come on Lofty. One of
the barns has a bit of the roof missing
and we're going to fix it!"

"Oh no!" whimpered Lofty.

Bob, Scoop, Muck and Dizzy arrived at the old cottage. They couldn't believe their eyes when they saw the mess Spud had made.

"Oh, no!" cried Bob. "We'd better sort the windows out before there is an accident."

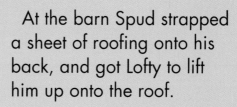

At the barn Spud strapped a sheet of roofing onto his back, and got Lofty to lift him up onto the roof.

"This is exciting," he said.

"Please be careful, Spud!" pleaded Lofty.

"Don't you worry," laughed Spud. "This is a job for Spud the Spanner!"

Just then a huge gust of wind blew him off the roof! Spud sailed through the air.

"H-E-L-P! Please, Lofty!" cried Spud as the wind blew him on.

Back at the old cottage, Muck looked up at the sky.

"What's that?" he wondered.

"Wow!" Dizzy squeaked excitedly. "It looks like a flying Spud!"

They all stared up at Spud who was flying straight towards them.

"Whey! Arrrghh!" Spud cried as he landed on the chimney of the old cottage.

"Nice landing, Spud," chuckled Bob.

Bob said he would only get Spud down if he promised never to use his tools again.

"Ummm, I'm sorry, Bob," mumbled Spud.

"And where's my toolbox?" asked Bob.

"Er, it's all right, Bob. I've got it," said Lofty as he came clanking up.

"Thank you, Lofty," said Bob. "Now you can get Spud down."

Lofty gently lowered Spud to the ground.

"I think I'll stay a scarecrow," Spud said. "It's much safer than being a builder!"

THE END!